Friends
fur-ever!

W9-AGD-011

This edition published by Parragon Books Ltd in 2014 and distributed by

Parragon Inc.
440 Park Avenue South, 13th Floor
New York, NY 10016
www.parragon.com

Copyright © Parragon Books Ltd 2013–2014

ISBN 978-1-4723-5201-9

Printed in China

Alice in Wonderland

Based on the original story
by Lewis Carroll
Retold by Catherine Allison

Illustrated by Erin McGuire

PaRragon

Bath • New York • Singapore • Hong Kong • Cologne • Delhi
Melbourne • Amsterdam • Johannesburg • Shenzhen

Alice was beginning to get very tired of sitting by her sister on the riverbank and of having nothing to do. It was hot, which made her feel very sleepy and slow. She was considering whether the pleasure of making a daisy chain would be worth the trouble of getting up and picking the daisies, when suddenly, a White Rabbit with pink eyes ran close by her.

There was nothing so very remarkable in that; nor did Alice think it so very unusual to hear the Rabbit say to itself, "Oh dear! Oh dear! I shall be too late!" But when the Rabbit actually took a watch out of its vest pocket, looked at it, and hurried on, Alice realized that she had never before seen a rabbit with either a vest pocket or a watch to take out of it. So she ran across the field after it and was just in time to see it pop into a large rabbit hole.

In another moment, in went Alice after it. The rabbit hole went straight on like a tunnel and then dipped suddenly down, and Alice found herself falling into what seemed like a deep well. It was too dark to see where she was falling to, but she could see that the sides of the well were filled with cupboards and bookshelves. She picked a jar labeled "Orange Marmalade" from one shelf. Sadly, it was empty, so she put it back.

Down and down she fell. There was nothing else to do, so Alice started thinking about her cat. "Dinah, my dear, I wish you were down here with me!"

Alice felt that she was dozing off and had just begun to dream, when suddenly, thump! Down she came on a heap of dry leaves, and the fall was over.

Alice jumped to her feet and saw the White Rabbit hurrying down a long passage ahead of her. There was not a moment to be lost. Away went Alice like the wind, just in time to hear it say, "Oh, my ears and whiskers, how late it's getting!" as it turned a corner. Then it disappeared from view.

Alice was now in a long, low hall with doors on all sides. They were all locked. In the center of the hall was a little, three-legged glass table, with a tiny golden key lying on it. It didn't fit any of the doors, but then Alice saw a low curtain that she had not noticed before. Behind it was a little door, only fifteen inches high. She tried the little golden key in the lock. It fitted!

Through the door, Alice could see the loveliest garden with bright flowers and cool fountains. How she longed to walk in it, but she could not even get her head through the doorway.

Feeling sad, Alice shut the door and went back to the glass table, only to find that a little bottle had appeared. Around its neck was a paper label with the words "Drink me" on it. Alice hesitated a moment, but then took a sip. It tasted of cherry tart, custard, pineapple, roast turkey, toffee, and hot buttered toast, and Alice very soon finished it off.

"What a curious feeling!" said Alice, as she shrank to only ten inches high. Now she could fit through the little door into the lovely garden, but alas, the key was still on the glass table, and she was much too small to reach it. Then her eye fell on a little glass box lying under the table. Inside was a very small cake with "Eat me" written on it. Alice took a bite and then another, until she finished it and had grown all over again.

"Curiouser and curiouser!" cried Alice. "Goodbye, feet!" She looked down, and her feet seemed to be almost out of sight. At the same time, her head struck against the roof of the hall. In fact, she was now more than nine feet high! She took up the little golden key and hurried off to the garden door.

Poor Alice! It was as much as she could do, lying down on one side, to look through to the garden with one eye; but to get through was more hopeless than ever. She sat down and began to cry. And though she tried to stop herself, she went on crying, shedding gallons of tears, until there was a large pool all around her, about four inches deep.

After a time, she heard a little pattering of feet in the distance. It was the White Rabbit returning, splendidly dressed, with a pair of soft, white leather gloves in one hand and a large fan in the other. Alice called out, "If you please, sir," which frightened the Rabbit so much that he jumped violently, dropped the gloves and the fan, and scurried away as fast as he could go.

Alice took up the fan and gloves. The hall was very hot, so she fanned herself again and again. When she looked down at her hands, she was surprised to see that she had put on one of the Rabbit's little white gloves. "I must be growing small again," she thought. She dropped the fan hastily, which she realized was the cause of her shrinking, just in time to avoid disappearing altogether.

Suddenly, her foot slipped, the gloves went flying, and splash! She was up to her chin in salt water, the gloves floating beside her. At first, she thought that she had somehow fallen into the sea, but she soon figured out that she was in the pool of tears that she had wept when she was nine feet high. "I wish I hadn't cried so much!" said Alice, as she swam to the shore and then did her best to get dry.

In a little while, the White Rabbit appeared again. "Where can I have dropped them, I wonder?" he muttered anxiously. Alice guessed that he was missing his fan and gloves.

Then the Rabbit noticed Alice and called out to her in an angry tone, "Mary Ann! Run home this moment and fetch me a pair of gloves and a fan!" Alice was so much frightened that she ran off at once in the direction he pointed to.

"He mistook me for his housemaid," she said to herself as she ran.

Soon she came upon a neat little house with "W. Rabbit" engraved on a bright brass plaque beside the door. She went in, hurried up the stairs, and found a table in the window with a fan and a pair of tiny white leather gloves on it. She took them up and was just going to leave, when her eye fell upon a little bottle near the looking glass. Alice uncorked it and put it to her lips. Before she had drunk half the bottle, she found her head pressing against the ceiling and had to stoop to save her neck from folding over. She went on growing, and as a last resort, she put one arm out of the window and one foot up the chimney.

After a few minutes, the White Rabbit came to the door and tried to open it, but Alice's elbow was pressed hard against it. He then decided to climb in through the window. "That you won't!" thought Alice, and she waved her hand about. There was a little shriek as the Rabbit fell off his ladder.

The next moment, a shower of little pebbles came rattling in at the window. As Alice watched, they turned into little cakes. In the hope that eating a cake would make her smaller, she swallowed one and was delighted to find that she began shrinking. As soon as she was small enough to get through the door, she ran out of the house and away as fast as she could.

Alice soon found herself in dense woods and began searching for something to eat or drink to make her grow again. There was a large mushroom near her, about the same height as herself, and when she had looked under it, on both sides of it, and behind it, it occurred to her that she might as well see what was on top of it. She peeped over the edge, and her eyes immediately met those of a large, blue caterpillar, sitting with its arms folded.

"Who are you?" said the Caterpillar.

"I—I hardly know, sir," Alice replied shyly. "I know who I was when I got up this morning, but I have changed several times since then. I don't keep the same size for ten minutes at a time."

"What size do you want to be?" it asked.

"Well, I should like to be a little larger," said Alice. "Three inches is such a wretched height to be."

"It's a very good height indeed!" said the Caterpillar angrily, rearing up. (It was exactly three inches high.)

Then it got down off the mushroom and crawled away, remarking as it went, "One side of the mushroom will make you grow taller, and the other side will make you grow shorter."

Alice broke off a piece of mushroom from each side and nibbled a little of the right-hand side. The next moment, her chin had struck her foot! She at once nibbled some of the other side. But alas! All of a sudden, her neck was immensely long, like a snake! So she carefully nibbled, first a piece from one side of the mushroom and then a piece from the other until she was her usual height. And then, seeing a little house ahead of her, she nibbled some more mushroom until she had brought herself down to eight inches high and was the right size to meet the owners.

As Alice approached the house, a messenger came running out of the woods and knocked loudly at the door. Then he handed a letter, nearly as large as himself, to a servant, saying in a solemn tone, "For the Duchess. An invitation from the Queen to play croquet."

There was the most extraordinary noise going on inside the house—a constant howling and sneezing, and every now and then, a great crash, as if a dish had been broken to pieces. But Alice was intent on going inside, so she slipped past the servant and stepped through the door.

She found herself in a large kitchen. The Duchess was sitting in the middle holding a baby, and a cook was stirring a large cauldron of soup over the fire. The air was full of pepper, which made Alice, the Duchess, and the baby sneeze (when the baby wasn't howling). The only things in the kitchen that were not sneezing were the cook and a large cat that was sitting on the hearth and grinning from ear to ear.

"Why does your cat grin like that?" Alice asked the Duchess timidly.

"It's a Cheshire Cat," snapped the Duchess, "and that's why."

Suddenly, the cook began throwing everything within her reach at the Duchess and the baby: a large ladle, then a shower of saucepans, plates, and dishes. The Duchess took no notice, even when they hit her, and the baby was howling so much already that it was quite impossible to say whether the blows hurt it or not.

"Here! You may hold it for a while, if you like!" the Duchess said to Alice, flinging the baby at her. "I must get ready to play croquet with the Queen." And with that, she departed. The baby snorted and grunted in the most alarming way, and looking at it more closely, Alice saw that it was, in fact, a small pig. It would be quite absurd for her to hold it any longer, she thought, so she set the little creature down and watched it trot away into the woods.

Once outside the house, Alice was a little startled to see the Cheshire Cat sitting on the bough of a tree. The Cat grinned when it saw Alice. It looked good-natured, she thought, but she still felt that it ought to be treated with respect.

"Cheshire Cat," she began. "Would you tell me, please, which way I ought to go from here?"

"That depends a lot on where you want to get to," said the Cat.

Alice felt that this could not be denied, so she tried another question. "What sort of people live around here?"

"In that direction," the Cat said, waving its right paw, "lives a Hatter. And in that direction"—it waved the other paw—"lives a March Hare. Visit whichever you like. They're both mad."

"But I'm not sure I want to go among mad people," Alice remarked.

"Oh, you can't help that," said the Cat. "We're all mad here. Do you play croquet with the Queen today?"

"I should like to play very much," said Alice, "but I haven't been invited yet."

Suddenly, the Cat vanished.

Alice was not much surprised at this, as she was getting so used to odd things happening. She waited a little, half expecting to see the Cat again, but it did not appear, so she walked on in the direction that the March Hare was said to live.

"I've seen hatters before," she thought, "so the March Hare should be much more interesting."

As she said this, she looked up, and there was the Cat on the branch again. After a moment, the Cat vanished again—quite slowly, beginning with the end of its tail and ending with its grin, which remained some time after the rest of it had gone.

Alice walked a little way farther and then came in sight of the March Hare's house. At least, she thought it was his house because the chimneys were shaped like ears and the roof was thatched with fur.

There was a table set out under a tree, and the March Hare and the Hatter were having tea at it. A Dormouse was sitting between them, fast asleep, and the other two were talking over its head. The table was a large one, but the three were all crowded together at one corner of it.

"No room! No room!" they cried out when Alice approached.

"There's plenty of room!" said Alice indignantly, and she sat down in a large armchair at one end of the table.

"Why is a raven like a writing desk?" asked the Hatter.

Alice sat silently for a minute while she pondered the riddle. She thought over all she could remember about ravens and writing desks, which wasn't much.

"I give up," said Alice. "What's the answer?"

"I haven't the slightest idea," said the Hatter.

Alice sighed wearily. "I think you might do something better with your time than waste it asking riddles with no answers."

The Hatter shook his head mournfully. "If you knew Time as well as I do, you wouldn't talk about wasting it. Time is a him, in any case. I quarreled with Time last March, and ever since that, he won't do a thing I ask! It's always six o'clock now."

"Is that the reason so many tea things are put out here?" Alice asked.

"Yes, that's it," said the Hatter with a sigh. "It's always teatime. We've no time to wash dishes, so instead we have our tea, move around the table to new seats with clean dishes, and have tea again." As he spoke, they all moved around.

"This is the stupidest tea party I ever was at in all my life," thought Alice. "I'll never come here again!"

And with that, she got up and walked off.

Ahead of her, Alice could see a tree with a door leading right into it. Stepping inside, she found herself back in the long hall with the little glass table, the golden key, and the door to the lovely garden. She nibbled some mushroom (she had kept a piece of it in her pocket) till she was about a foot high, then walked through the door and into the garden.

In front of her was a large rose tree with white roses on it. Three gardeners were busily painting them red.

"Would you tell me," said Alice, "why you are painting those roses?"

"This ought to have been a red rose tree, miss," said one, "and we put a white one in by mistake. If the Queen were to find out, we should all have our heads cut off."

Suddenly, another gardener called out, "The Queen! The Queen!" and all three gardeners instantly threw themselves flat upon their faces.

A procession approached, made up of the Knave of Hearts, a platoon of soldiers made of playing cards, and the King and Queen of Hearts last of all.

When the Queen saw what the gardeners had done, she shouted, "Off with their heads!" then walked away. Before the soldiers knew what was happening, Alice helped the gardeners hide in a large flowerpot nearby. After a few minutes of searching, the soldiers gave up and marched off in the direction of the Queen. Alice decided to follow them to the croquet ground.

Alice had never seen such a curious croquet ground in all her life. The balls were live hedgehogs, the mallets were live flamingos, and the soldiers had to stand on all fours to make the arches. Even when Alice had succeeded in getting her flamingo's body tucked away under her arm and its neck nicely straightened out, it would twist itself around and look up in her face with a puzzled expression, which made her laugh.

And when she had got its head down to strike a hedgehog, the hedgehog unrolled itself and crawled away. It was a very difficult game, indeed! Alice decided to escape without the Queen noticing.

Very soon, Alice came upon a Gryphon.

"Have you seen the Mock Turtle yet?" it asked.

"No," said Alice. "I never saw one. I don't even know what a Mock Turtle is."

"Come on then," said the Gryphon, "and he shall tell you his history."

They had not gone far before they saw the Mock Turtle, sitting sad and lonely on a little ledge of rock. As they came nearer, Alice could hear him sighing as if his heart would break.

"Why is he sad?" she asked the Gryphon.

"It's all his fancy, that," said the creature. "He's got no sorrow, you know." Then it turned to the Mock Turtle. "This here young lady wants to know your history, she do," it said.

"I'll tell it her," said the Mock Turtle.

There followed a long silence, broken only by the Mock Turtle's constant heavy sobbing.

"When we were little," it said at last, more calmly, "we went to school in the sea. The master was an old Turtle. We used to call him Tortoise."

"Why did you call him Tortoise, if he wasn't one?" Alice asked.

"We called him Tortoise because he taught us," said the Mock Turtle angrily. "Really, you are very stupid!"

"And how many hours a day did you do lessons?" said Alice.

"Ten hours the first day," said the Mock Turtle, "nine the next, and so on."

"What a curious plan!" exclaimed Alice.

"That's the reason they're called lessons," the Gryphon remarked, "because they lessen from day to day."

All at once, a cry of "The trial's beginning!" was heard in the distance.

"What trial is it?" asked Alice, but the Gryphon only answered, "Come on!" Then he took her by the hand and ran.

The King and Queen of Hearts were seated on their thrones when Alice arrived, with a great crowd around them—all sorts of little birds and beasts as well as the whole pack of cards. The Knave was standing in front of them in chains, and nearby was the White Rabbit, holding a trumpet and a scroll of parchment. The King was the judge, wearing a wig under his crown, and there were twelve jurors in a jury box, who were a mixture of animals and birds. In the very middle of the court was a table with tarts upon it.

"Silence in the court!" the White Rabbit cried out.

"Herald, read the accusation!" said the King.

The Rabbit blew three blasts on the trumpet, unrolled the parchment scroll, and read as follows:

"The Queen of Hearts, she made some tarts,

All on a summer day.

The Knave of Hearts, he stole those tarts,

And took them clean away!"

"Consider your verdict," the King said to the jury.

"Not yet, not yet!" the Rabbit hastily interrupted. "There's a lot to come before that!"

"Call the first witness," said the King, and the White Rabbit called out, "The Hatter!"

The Mad Hatter came in with a teacup in one hand and a piece of bread and butter in the other.

"I beg pardon, your Majesty, but I hadn't quite finished my tea when I was sent for."

"Give your evidence," said the King, "and don't be nervous, or I'll have you executed on the spot."

Just at this moment, Alice felt a very curious sensation. She was beginning to grow larger again.

"I'm a poor man, your Majesty," said the Hatter miserably.

"You're a very poor speaker," said the King. "You may go. Call the next witness!"

Alice leapt up in surprise when the White Rabbit read out, "Alice!"

"Here I am!" cried Alice. She jumped up in a hurry, quite forgetting how large she had grown in the last few minutes, and tipped over the jury box with the edge of her skirt. The jurors flew out.

"Oh, I beg your pardon," she exclaimed.

When the jurors were back in their seats, the King said to Alice, "What do you know about this business?"

"Nothing," said Alice.

"Nothing whatever?" persisted the King.

"Nothing whatever," said Alice.

Then the King read out from a book, "Rule forty-two. All persons more than a mile high to leave the court."

Everybody looked at Alice.

"I'm not a mile high," said Alice.

"You are," said the King.

"Nearly two miles high," added the Queen.

"Well, I shan't go, at any rate," said Alice. "You invented that rule just now."

The King turned pale. "Consider your verdict," he said to the jury.

"No, no!" said the Queen. "Sentence first, verdict afterward."

"Stuff and nonsense!" said Alice loudly. "The idea of having the sentence first!"

"Hold your tongue!" said the Queen, turning purple.

"I won't!" said Alice.

"Off with her head!" the Queen shouted at the top of her voice.

"Who cares for you?" said Alice (who had grown to her full size by this time). "You're nothing but a pack of cards!"

At this, the whole pack rose up into the air and flew down upon her. She gave a little scream and tried to beat them off. The next moment, she found herself lying on the bank with her head in the lap of her sister, who was gently brushing away some dead leaves that had fluttered down from the trees upon her face.

"Wake up, Alice dear!" said her sister. "What a long sleep you've had!"

"I've had such a curious dream!" said Alice, and she told her sister all her strange adventures. Then she ran off home for tea, thinking while she ran, as well she might, what a wonderful dream it had been.